School Is A Nightmare #5

Winter Breakdown

RAYMOND BEAN

ISBN: 1481106333
ISBN 13: 9781481106337

www.raymondbean.com

Raymond Bean books

Baseball: A Ticket to the Bigs

Sweet Farts Series
Sweet Farts #1
Sweet Farts #2 Rippin' It Old School
Sweet Farts #3 Blown Away

School Is A Nightmare Series
School Is A Nightmare #1
First Week, Worst Week
School Is A Nightmare #2 The Field Trip
School Is A Nightmare #3 Shocktober
School Is A Nightmare #4
Yuck Mouth and the Thanksgiving Miracle
School Is A Nightmare – Quadzilla
(Books 1-4) Special Edition
School Is A Nightmare #5
Winter Breakdown (Coming Fall 2013)
School Is A Nightmare #6 Cupid's Crush
(Coming Winter 2014)

For Stacy, Ethan, and Chloe

Interested in scheduling an
author visit or web based author talk?
Email us at raymondbeanbooks@gmail.com

Contents

1
The Powdered Sugar Situation

If you ask me, winter break is by far the best break of the entire school year. I get a bunch of days off, a ton of presents, and I stay up super late on New Year's Eve. The final Friday before the start of the break had finally arrived after weeks of waiting, and my class party was in full swing when *it* happened.

A bunch of the moms came in to make a craft and feed us a ton of holiday snacks. There were so many different types of holiday cookies it was ridiculous. By the middle of the craft, the energy level in the class was through the roof.

I was about three cookies in when Bobby Thorton said, "I can totally eat more cookies than you."

"You wish," I said, popping another into my mouth.

"What do you want to bet?" he asked.

"I guess that depends on what you're prepared to lose," I said confidently.

Bobby Thorton was new to the school and way more fun than the rest of the kids in my class. He held up a five-dollar bill. "Five bucks," he mumbled, his mouth full of cookie.

"Five bucks it is," I mumbled back.

My teacher, the dreaded Mrs. Cliff, passed by our desks and gave me a dirty look. I smiled, my cheeks bulging with cookie.

"Don't overdo it, boys," she warned.

"No need to worry, Mrs. Cliff," Bobby assured her.

"I'm glad you're having fun, Bobby," she said, walking toward the other side of the room.

Bobby was too new to fully appreciate how awful she was. It had only been about two weeks since he moved to our school. Mrs. Cliff really enjoyed the holiday season, and she'd been especially nice for the weeks he'd been in the class. I tried to warn him not to get used to it. He'd get to know the real Mrs. Cliff after the holidays passed.

"I don't know why you don't like her. She's pretty awesome if you ask me," he said.

I almost choked on my gingerbread man. "Give it some time. What you're seeing is holiday cheer."

"I don't know. She's been really nice to me."

"Let's talk around Martin Luther King Day in January. I'm sure you'll be ready to move back to wherever you came from by then."

Bobby laughed, and the powdered sugar on his cookie puffed out a tiny cloud of smoke.

"Awesome!" I said, picking up a powdered cookie from my plate and blowing on it. Another small powdered sugar cloud puffed out in front of us.

"Totally!" he said, blowing on his again.

The other kids at our table did the same, and before I knew it, kids all over the class were doing it too. The moms and Mrs. Cliff were too busy talking about their holiday plans to notice. I blew a puff toward Ben, who was sitting right across from me. He blew a puff back at me, and pretty soon, my entire table was blowing powdered sugar at each other. Without warning, they all turned on me and blew at the same time. A massive cloud of sugar filled the air. I breathed in a sweet gulp that choked me. They blew another cloud, and I hit the deck, trying to hide under my table, but instead I smacked my chin off the edge of my desk and fell to the floor.

It's funny how a class can change from complete craziness to complete silence in the blink of an eye when someone gets hurt. I must have hit my chin pretty hard because I don't really remember falling to the floor. One second I was in my chair, and the next I was down with the pencil shavings and Mrs. Cliff was helping me up.

"What's going on over here?" she barked.

"He smacked his chin off the desk pretty hard," Bobby said.

"You're lucky you didn't really hurt yourself," she said. "I don't appreciate that you've turned Mrs. Blane's powdered sugar cookies into a toy."

"It wasn't just me!" I pleaded. "Everyone was doing it."

The kids at my table looked shocked. Ben's mouth dropped as though he'd seen a ghost, and Bobby's eyes bulged out like a frog's.

"Don't act so surprised, guys. You know you were doing it too," I said.

"It's not that," Bobby said. "You totally cracked your front tooth!"

I ran my finger along the place where my front tooth used to be, and a big chunk was missing.

"Take him to the nurse!" Mrs. Cliff shouted.

2
She's the Worst

By the time I returned from the nurse, the party was over, and the cookies were all gone. The only thing left on my desk was a thin layer of powdered sugar. My mom and dad were both at work, and it would take them at least an hour to pick me up and bring me to the dentist.

The class was working on a reading packet about different winter holidays. It was *really* thick! The kids were super quiet and working way too hard for the day before the winter break.

"What's this all about?" I whispered to Bobby, pointing at the packet.

Mrs. Cliff appeared behind me out of nowhere like the Grim Reaper. "That's our winter break assignment," she answered. "How is your tooth?"

"It's fine. The nurse said my mom is going to pick me up at the end of the day to take me to the dentist. Do we have to finish this whole thing before we leave today?" I asked.

"Of course not," she said, smiling.

"Thank goodness. I thought you were going say we had to do it all today."

"No, you have until January second to complete the assignment."

My heart almost stopped. I flipped through the packet. It had to be thirty pages, *double-sided*! The other kids didn't even look up, they were so busy working.

"I don't think so," I said. Immediately I knew I'd made a mistake.

"Excuse me?" Mrs. Cliff said, narrowing her eyes.

"I don't think my parents are going to be cool with this. We'll be pretty busy over the break."

"You can make time," she said, her eyes squinting the way they do when she's annoyed.

"What happens if I don't get it done?" I asked.

"Failure is not an option," she said. "It contains a plethora of interesting holiday information from cultures around the world. There's some great reading and a little research you'll need to complete. Without that packet, your worldview of winter holidays around the world will be utterly limited."

"Research!" I blurted out.

I didn't hear a word of the other stuff she mentioned, but *research?* I couldn't believe my own ears. Bobby kicked me under the desk to snap me out of the certain destruction awaiting me. I ignored it. I'd waited months for the winter break to arrive, and Mrs. Cliff expected me to spend it finishing a mountain of work for her. I ran my tongue along my cracked tooth again, and something in me snapped.

"I told you she's awful," I whispered to Bobby, but not quite low enough, because everyone, including Mrs. Cliff, heard me. An eerie silence fell over the class like in a horror movie right before something jumps out at you.

"Are you referring to me?" Mrs. Cliff asked.

The silence deepened. No one took a breath.

There was a split second for me to recover and make up some excuse. I should have said something like "Of course not" or "Don't be silly" or anything else that would have kept me out of trouble, but I was beyond the point of return. I'd lost touch with clear thought and common sense, so I didn't say anything like that at all.

Instead, I said, "You bet!"

Mrs. Cliff looked like a volcano ready to blow its top. If it were a cartoon, black smoke would have whistled out of her ears.

3
Hum

When Mom picked me up at the end of the
day, I was sitting in the "trouble chair" in
the office while Mom talked with Mrs. Cliff and
then the nurse. It was terrible because everyone
else seemed to be in the best moods ever as they
marched out to the buses and got picked up by
their parents.

My sisters, Becky and Mindy, sat on either
side of me.

"Unbelievable!" Becky said.

"Truly!" Mindy replied.

"Let's see the tooth," Becky said.

I didn't look at her.

"You'll have to show us sooner or later," Mindy said.

"I guess we know what you'll be asking for for Christmas this year," Becky said.

"Seriously! I know you like the song 'All I Want for Christmas Is My Two Front Teeth,' but this is ridiculous," Mindy said, chuckling, when Mom appeared with Mrs. Cliff.

"Justin, I think you have something you want to say to Mrs. Cliff," she said, nodding toward her.

The girls were eating it up. Here they were, witnessing one of my most embarrassing moments and loving every minute of it.

"Justin," Mom repeated. "We're waiting."

"I shouldn't have said that. I'm sorry," I said, noticing that every time I made the *s* sound, my tooth whistled. The girls covered their mouths to keep from laughing.

"I accept your apology. The holiday stress can get the best of us sometimes," Mrs. Cliff said. "I hope you have a nice holiday and hope your tooth is fixed up like new."

I couldn't believe she was so nice and forgiving. It wasn't like her.

"Again, I'm so incredibly sorry, Mrs. Cliff," Mom said. "Justin's father and I will handle this, and Justin will be punished appropriately at home. We wish you a happy holiday." She turned toward me. "*Let's go,* Justin."

Mom walked ahead of me down the path leading to the parking lot. The girls walked behind me humming "All I Want for Christmas Is My Two Front Teeth."

4
Christmas Bust

Mom drove me straight to the dentist. The four of us sat in the waiting room for what seemed like forever. I couldn't believe how many people were at the dentist on the Friday before Christmas. The place was absolutely packed.

By the time they called me, it was almost five o'clock. Mom hadn't said a word to me since we left the school. I knew that the longer Mom gave me the silent treatment, the worse my situation. She'd been mad at me in the past, but not like this. I'd definitely reached a new level of anger and frustration with her.

"What seems to be the problem, Justin?" the dentist said when it was finally my turn, pointing to the chair.

"I chipped my tooth at school."

"Let's have a look," she said, so I hopped into the chair and opened up.

Mom was shaking her head in disbelief, and the girls were still covering their mouths to keep from laughing.

"How'd you pull that off?" the dentist asked.

"Powdered sugar," I said, and the way "sugar" whistled out of me made the girls lose it and burst out laughing. I think the dentist may have laughed a bit too.

Then Mom said, "We've had a long day, and with the holidays only a few days away, we need Justin's tooth fixed today. Can you do it?"

"I can do my best, but he'll have to be really careful with what he eats. Anything chewy or really hard will pull the cap I'm putting in right back out. Since it's a permanent tooth, this is something you'll have for the rest of your life, Justin."

Mom looked as if she might faint. She shook her head some more and sat down on the chair against the wall. "How much is this going to cost?" she asked.

"Probably about five hundred, but we can put you on a payment plan if you don't want to pay today," the dentist said.

That's when Mom finally spoke to me. "Well, Justin, would you like to pay in cash, or should they put you on a payment plan?"

"Me?" I asked.

"You were the one who managed to chip your front tooth eating a cookie at a holiday party. You were the one who decided today was a good day to insult your teacher in front of the entire class. So, yes, I am asking you how *you* would like to pay for this."

The girls looked as if they might burst.

"Don't you think we should talk to Dad about this first?" I asked.

"No, I don't," Mom said. "You're paying, kiddo."

"Can't I leave it?" I asked. "It's not that bad." I grinned into the mirror next to my chair. It was pretty bad, but I didn't want to admit it.

"It's *that* bad," Mindy said.

"Complete disaster," Becky added.

"Cash or payment plan?" the dentist asked. "I have a jammed lobby out there."

I lay back in the chair, giving up. "Bill me," I said and opened wide.

"Maybe you can sell some of your Christmas presents to help pay for it," Mindy said.

I wanted to say something, but luckily for her, the dentist's fingers were already in my mouth. It was not how I'd expected to spend the first hour of the winter break.

Becky took a picture of me when Mom wasn't looking. "For the holiday photo album," she teased.

5
Whistling Bill

That night when we got home, I went straight to my room.

"No video games or TV," my mom called. "You're grounded until further notice. Why don't you get started on that packet Mrs. Cliff wants you to complete?"

"No!" I called back. "It's the first night of the break. I need to relax. Plus, my tooth hurts." I exaggerated. It felt a little weird, but it didn't really hurt.

"You're working on that packet tonight or going straight to bed!"

"Fine!" I plunked down into my desk chair and opened the packet. I tried to read the first article about how different cultures around the world have different traditions for Christmas, but there was no way to focus. My mind kept replaying what I'd said to Mrs. Cliff.

After about an hour, I went downstairs and sat at the counter in the kitchen.

"What were you thinking?" Dad asked, taking a bite out of his apple.

"Don't ask."

"Who does that? Do other kids talk that way to their teachers?" he asked.

"Nope!" Becky interrupted.

"I've never heard of such disrespect," Mindy said.

"Cut it out!" I demanded.

"That's enough, girls," Mom said. "Give me and your father a few minutes alone with your brother, Whistling Bill."

The girls ran for the back door and went outside to play.

"It really wasn't that big of a deal," I said.

"It was absolutely a big deal," Mom disagreed.

"You're grounded until Christmas. That's a pretty big deal in my book," Dad said. "I spoke with Mrs. Cliff after work. She was really upset and thinks you have a problem with authority."

"I don't," I said, wondering what that even means.

"She thinks you can't handle it when you don't get your way and you have a problem following rules. Were you really having a cookie-eating contest when you chipped your tooth?"

"Yeah, but it wasn't my idea."

"It doesn't matter whose idea it was," Mom said. "You should know better. Who has a cookie-eating contest at a holiday party anyway?"

I decided it was better to simply listen. My parents were really mad, and when they get that upset, there's nothing I can say that will make it better. I know I'm not going to change their minds, so I listen and nod a lot. Sometimes my dad goes on and on and on, and I just keep nodding and try to make eye contact to make it look I'm listening, but I'm not.

They seemed to be talking forever. Their voices blended into a mumble until I heard the words "return some of your Christmas presents."

"What's that now?" I asked, returning to the conversation.

"We're going to have to return some of the things we bought you for Christmas," Mom said. "You can't behave like you did and then expect to go without a punishment. Your timing couldn't be worse."

"I'll take a punishment, but don't take away my gifts! It's Christmas, for goodness sake."

"Sorry, pal. Your mother's right. If you're talking back to teachers in fourth grade, who knows what you'll be up to in middle school and high school? Expect a light Christmas from us this year."

I've had some pretty bad punishments over the years, but this was off-the-charts bad. It didn't even seem like something parents could do. It was as if they were canceling Christmas.

6
When Are We Leaving?

On Christmas Eve, Grandma arrived. She always stays with us for about a week around Christmas.

"Can you be a dear and run out to the car and grab Grandma's bags?" she asked.

"Sure, Grandma," I said, and ran for her car. I clicked the button on her key chain that popped the trunk. It was full of luggage. When I moved the first bag, I noticed a bunch of shopping bags. One was labeled "Justin." I couldn't help myself, and I pulled open the bag and peeked inside. On top was a pack of socks. Below that, there was a pair of flip-flops, a bathing suit, and a pair of swim goggles. My heart skipped a beat when I heard the squeak of the front door. After pulling two suitcases out of the trunk, I headed back toward the door.

Grandma opened it to let me into the house. "My big, strong man," she said, tousling my hair as I walked by. "I hope you didn't look in the shopping bags out there."

"Where would you like these bags?" I asked, changing the subject.

"You can set them down right here by the door."

"Won't you need them in your room?" I asked.

"I'm not staying long enough to unpack this year," she said with a wink. "Trust me. Leave them here."

"You're staying for Christmas tomorrow, aren't you?"

"Perhaps."

"When are you leaving?"

"The question isn't when I'm leaving, but when we're leaving." She snickered.

"What do you mean? We're staying home for Christmas this year."

"We'll see," she said with a grin.

7
Hogwash

All night I tried to get Grandma to tell me what she was talking about, but she wouldn't budge. It was a pretty normal Christmas Eve. We decorated the tree, a few people from the neighborhood came over to visit, and the girls begged for presents.

We stayed up with Grandma and watched a movie. It was about this kid who wants a BB gun for Christmas. I thought it was pretty funny because my mom won't even let me have a water gun. I can't even imagine her letting me get a

BB gun. I asked Grandma if she'd get me one, and she said maybe for my birthday.

"Your dad had one when he was eight," she said.

I looked at Dad. "You had one at eight, and I can't have one now? That hardly seems fair."

"Things were different back then," Mom said.

"Yes, we walked uphill both ways, it snowed every day, and everyone was armed. Be happy with your modern life. You can't have a BB gun in our neighborhood. Someone would call the police."

"I still kind of want one."

"Forget it," Mom said. "You can get one when you're forty. For now, just be happy you'll be getting anything at all."

"Why wouldn't he be getting anything?" Grandma asked, pulling me closer and giving me a squeeze. "He should get everything he wants. He's an angel!"

"He wasn't such an angel at school," Dad said.

"Hogwash," Grandma said. "He's a perfect boy."

Mindy and Becky sat down on the floor by the fireplace, in front of Grandma and me.

"Would a perfect boy tell his teacher she's awful?" Becky asked.

"Did you do that?" Grandma asked, grabbing my face and squeezing my cheeks like she was trying to pop them.

"I kind of did."

"He also kind of cracked his tooth on his desk because he was playing some childish cookie-eating game," Mindy tattled.

"He should be childish. He's a child. When I was a kid, I was an absolute terror, and I turned out all right."

"You were?" I asked.

"Oh yeah," Grandma said. "I was a real handful. But your father was the real teacher terror. I was at that principal's office so much with him when he was younger I thought about getting a job in the school to save on gas."

Dad looked pretty uncomfortable. "Let's change the subject," he suggested. "Tomorrow's Christmas, and these guys need their rest."

For the first time in a long time, Becky, Mindy, and I all agreed. Grandma should continue her story. We were practically begging when she stood and pulled three small presents from her bag.

"I agree with your father. Let's change the subject. He was a wonderful kid, and he never got in trouble. Forget I said anything."

"What's in the boxes?" I asked.

"I say we find out!" she said.

"I don't know," Mom said. "It's kind of late, and the kids really need to get up pretty early tomorrow."

Grandma smirked. "You'll have to get up early too."

"What do you mean?" Mom said. "I've been working like a dog all week. I need to relax tomorrow morning."

"Oh, you'll be relaxed," Grandma said, smiling.

"What are you getting at, Mom?" Dad asked. "You're acting a little strange."

"Let's let the kids open these presents, and then I think it will all make sense," she said.

Mom and Dad gave each other a look and finally agreed. Grandma handed each of us a present and squeaked a little with excitement. Mom and Dad nodded that it was all right.

"OK," Grandma said, "Mindy, then Becky, and then Justin. Open them in that order, and let's have some fun."

Mindy tore into her present. It was a small box with a magazine cutout of a black stretch limo.

"You bought me a limousine!" she shouted.

"Not quite, sweetie. Be patient. Your sister and brother still have to go."

Becky opened her present, and it was a magazine cutout of a hotel on the beach.

"What's going on, Mom?" Dad asked.

"Wait for it," she said. "Your turn, Justin."

I opened my present, and it was a gift box. Inside were six airplane tickets to Aruba.

"We're going on vacation!" Grandma shouted. "Pack your bags and grab the sunscreen because we'll be poolside this Christmas."

We all just kind of sat there, not sure what to say. Finally Mom said, "That sounds wonderful, but when are we leaving?"

"Tomorrow morning at six a.m. It will be the adventure of a lifetime. You guys are so busy and caught up in everything here with your work and your school. You've got to live a little, and I want to spend some time with my grandkids."

"Mom, we can't leave tomorrow. It's Christmas," Dad said.

"I know, but this is a once-in-a-lifetime trip. I got a deal that would blow your mind."

Mom, Dad, and Grandma moved the conversation into the kitchen so we wouldn't hear them arguing. The girls and I sat silently for a few seconds, confused by what had just happened, when Becky said, "I'm going to pack," and ran toward her room.

"Do you think we're really going on vacation tomorrow?" I asked Mindy.

"Mom and Dad didn't seem too thrilled about the idea, but if Grandma wants to go, I'll bet we're going."

I'd never been to Aruba, but I knew I'd love it. Warm weather, tropical beaches, and pools, what's not to love?

After a while, the grown-ups came out of the kitchen. They called Mindy back down to the living room, and Dad said, "Well, your grandma really threw us a curveball with this vacation. We have a choice to make. We can either cancel the trip, and Grandma will lose a bunch of money, or we can go."

"Let's go," the girls said at practically the same time.

"What about Christmas tomorrow?" I asked.

"Our flight's at six," Mom said. "If we're going to make it, we'd have to leave around three in the morning. We'd have to put Christmas off until after we get back."

"Postpone Christmas?" Mindy said, sounding less interested than before.

"Your presents will be here waiting for you when you get back, but we'll have a week in the sun and sand. It's a once-in-a-lifetime opportunity, kids. Who's up for an adventure?"

The room was silent as everyone thought about going on vacation instead of Christmas.

"It's not what we planned, but it's very generous, and I'm sure we'll have a blast. I say we go," Mom said. "Who knows when we'll get a chance to go on vacation again?"

"If you're in, then so am I," Dad said.

The girls nodded that they were in too.

"I guess I can call Aaron and ask him to take care of my pets while we're away," I said.

"All right then," Grandma said. "Go put away your coats and hats, and go grab your sunglasses and bathing suits. We're going to the islands for Christmas!"

8
Git Up

At three o'clock in the morning, my alarm clock went off, and I stumbled out of bed. I grabbed the backpack I'd packed the night before and ran downstairs. Mom and Dad were already in the kitchen. There were a bunch of suitcases by the front door, and I noticed a load of presents under the tree.

"Are you sure you're all right with this?" Mom asked.

"I guess so. Can we open our presents before we go?"

"Sorry, buddy," Dad said. "The car to the airport just pulled up. The presents will be here when we get back."

It was like torture seeing all the presents under the Christmas tree and not being able to open them, so I snuck over and started looking for anything with my name on it.

"Justin's peeking at the presents," Mindy shouted.

"No, I'm not. I'm just taking a look to get a sense of what we got. Looks like your stocking is loaded up with coal," I said.

"You wish. I should have bought you a coal stove this year because that's all you're going to get after what happened with your teacher."

Mom walked into the room. "You two better knock it off right now. We've got a long ride to the airport and then a long flight before we get where we're going. There's to be no arguing today."

"Yes, Mother," Mindy said sarcastically.

"Don't 'Yes, Mother' me," Mom warned. "I'm being serious. Cut it out, and let's get ready for some Christmas joy."

"The car's here," Becky called from the front window. "At least I think it's the car."

I ran to the window and noticed that the car in the driveway wasn't a limo like the magazine cutout Grandma had shown us. It was a big black van. The driver had parked in the driveway, and I could see him in the back of it cleaning up.

"That's not a limo," Becky pointed out.

"No, it's not," Grandma said.

"Well, it's time to go, so we'd better grab our things and figure this out," Dad said.

Everyone grabbed a bag, and we all scurried down the front steps toward the van. When we got closer, I could smell cigarette smoke. The driver climbed out the sliding side door. He looked like he'd just woken up or had been up all night. I couldn't tell. His hair was a mess, and he had on a wrinkled-up dress shirt and a crooked tie.

"Merry Christmas. My name is Norton," he said.

"Merry Christmas to you as well, Norton. My name is Mimi. You can call me Mim. We seem to have a little mix-up, Norton. This isn't a limo," Grandma said.

"You're entirely correct, Mimi. This is not a limousine. However, it is here, and your flight is in a few hours."

"What happened to the limo I reserved?" she asked.

"It is broken down on the side of the highway right now, I'm afraid. However, I think you'll find that this van is more comfortable than any limo you're going to find."

"I don't think we have a choice," Dad said. "It's late. We've got to go if we're going to make this flight."

Everyone agreed and climbed into the van. It was huge inside. Dad sat in the front with Norton. Mom and Grandma sat in the two big recliner-like chairs in the second row, behind Dad and Norton. The girls and I jammed into the long couch-like seat all the way in the back. Behind that was all of the luggage. It felt like we were in someone's stinky living room, but we were flying along the highway at about eighty miles per hour.

"Justin," Mom called from in front of me.

"Yeah?"

"You packed your bag last night like I asked you, right?"

"Yep, I'm all set. My bag's back there with the rest."

"You packed your flip-flops?"

"Umm..."

"You packed your shorts?"

"Not exactly..."

"Did you pack your short-sleeve shirts?"

I couldn't believe it. Mom had given me a list of stuff to pack the night before, and I had completely forgotten about it.

"I kind of forgot a bunch of stuff," I admitted.

"What did you pack?" Mom asked.

"I have a few bathing suits and a bunch of candy."

9
You Look Like You Got Punched

Mom went off on me for about ten minutes before she finally calmed down. She had been really big on responsibility lately. She wanted me to do more things for myself, and the fact that I failed to pack a simple backpack of clothes showed she had reason to worry.

The light in the van was pretty low, but I could see the girls in the light from the highway. I caught a glimpse of Mindy's face, and something didn't look right. I'd seen it before, when she'd had allergic reactions in the past. Her eyes swelled up as if she'd been the big loser in a box-ing match. She was sleeping, and her face was smooshed up in the cushion of the van seat.

"Mom," I said.

"I'm trying to get a little rest before we get to the airport, Justin. What is it?"

"I think Norton might have cats."

"What difference does it make if Norton has cats?"

"Because I think he might keep them in the van."

"Oh yeah," Norton called from the front. "I have three little pussycats running around somewhere in here. They usually hide under the seats when I'm driving folks."

Dad and Mom spun around instantly. "My daughter is allergic to cats," Dad said.

"Mindy," Mom called, trying to wake her. "Wake up, honey."

"Are we there yet?" she asked, lifting her head from the seat.

All of us let out a loud "Oohhhhh." Her face was completely puffed out.

She touched her eyes and started to freak out. "No! I can't go to the beach like this."

"Norton, don't you think you should tell people you have live cats in your van before they load their children into it?" Dad asked.

"How was I supposed to know that she was allergic?" he said.

"You weren't, but it would have been nice if you shared that information with us."

"Who's allergic to cats?" he asked.

"I am," Mindy called from the back.

"Huh, I never heard of that."

"You never heard of someone being allergic to cats?" Mom asked.

"Nope, never once. Must be very rare," Norton said.

I couldn't tell if he was being serious or kidding around. It was hard to imagine a grown man who'd never heard of cat allergies.

"Actually, loads of people are allergic to cats," Mindy shouted.

"Pull this bucket of bolts off at the next exit and get us to a pharmacy right away," Grandma ordered.

Norton slammed on the gas, and the van took off like a rocket ship. Becky pulled on her seat belt to tighten it, and it pulled right out of the seat.

"My seat belt ripped off!" she shouted, holding it in her hand.

"Yeah, that happens," Norton shouted back. "I'll have to screw it back on after you guys get to the airport. Don't worry. It's cool."

10
The Flight Fright

Luckily, Norton found a pharmacy that was open, and Mom was able to buy some allergy medicine for Mindy. Her eyes were really puffy, but at least she would survive the flight to Aruba.

I was so tired by the time we got to the airport that I was practically asleep on my feet. Before I knew it, we were on the plane. I realized I'd never really been on a plane before. I was on one once when I was three and we flew to Florida, but I hardly remembered it.

I was happy Grandma and I got to sit together. I even got the seat next to the window. The girls were seated way in the back with Mom, and Dad was seated all by himself toward the front.

"I hope this seat next to me stays empty," Grandma said, patting the aisle seat.

"That would be great," I said. As I said it, I realized I was already falling asleep. I didn't want to because I wanted to experience takeoff and they had a pretty cool movie that they were going to show. There was no stopping it. My eyes were heavy. Grandma was talking, and I couldn't follow what she was saying.

I must have fallen asleep because the next thing I knew, I was back at school. I was really uncomfortable in my chair, and Mrs. Cliff was rambling on about Aruba. She talked and talked about all the touristy places to go visit, all the good restaurants, and the wonderful beaches. I tossed and turned, trying to change my dream and think about something else, but I couldn't.

I finally opened my eyes when I heard the stewardess asking people if they'd like a drink. All of a sudden, I was so thirsty I could hardly take it anymore. I sat up and snapped out of my nightmare.

The plane was pretty dark. Grandma was asleep. A lot of people were sleeping or reading. It was hard to tell if I'd been asleep for ten minutes or an hour.

The stewardess was a really tall lady who leaned in and whispered, "Would you like a drink?"

"I'll have an orange juice, please," I said.

While she poured my orange juice, I peeked out the window and saw nothing but fluffy clouds as far as I could see.

"Here you go," she said.

I turned back to take it from her and realized that a woman was in the seat next to Grandma. Her head was turned toward the aisle, but she looked really familiar. I leaned over Grandma to get a better look, and the woman sat up, startling me, and said, "Good morning, Justin. How was your rest?"

I dropped my orange juice on the floor from shock. "Good morning, Mrs. Cliff."

11
Totally Unbelievable

Grandma woke up when my orange juice splashed on her leg. "Oh, Justin, you're up. Can you believe your teacher is sitting right here with us? I was going to wake you before, but you were sound asleep. What a surprise!"

"I totally can't believe it," I said, trying to fake a smile to be polite.

"When I sat down earlier, you were already asleep," Mrs. Cliff said. "How's your tooth?"

"It feels a little funny still, but it's better."

"Mrs. Cliff is staying at the same hotel as us!" Grandma said enthusiastically. "What are the odds that your teacher would be at the same hotel as us all the way in Aruba! She and I were really hitting it off before. She's a regular tourist guide. You'd be amazed at how much she knows about the island. Seriously, what are the odds?"

"It's got to be about a billion to one," I said. "Totally unbelievable. If you'll excuse me, I have to use the bathroom."

They both stood so I could make my way to the aisle and toward the bathroom in the back of the plane. When I got out to the aisle, I saw Dad sleeping. I walked down the aisle toward the bathroom and where Mom and the girls were seated. The girls were asleep, and Mom was reading.

I knelt down next to Mom, who was sitting on the aisle seat. "We have to stay at another hotel," I whispered.

"What are you talking about? The hotel Grandma booked looks lovely. I looked at it online last night."

"We can't stay there. I'll sleep on the beach if I have to, but don't make me stay there."

"What's gotten into you? I thought you were excited about this place."

"I was until I learned that Mrs. Cliff is staying there too!"

"That's ridiculous," Mom said.

"It's ridiculous, all right, but it's my reality. She's sitting up there next to Grandma. Can I parachute out of this plane?"

"Come on, Justin. It's a little early in the morning for pranks."

"Mom, she's up there, and she's staying at our hotel."

Just as Mom was about to get back to her book, Mrs. Cliff stood and took her bag down from the overhead compartment.

"You've got to be kidding me," Mom whispered. "What are the chances?"

"I changed my mind. I don't want to go away for Christmas anymore," I said.

12
Gertrude

The rest of the flight, I pretended to sleep, but I couldn't. By the time we landed, Mrs. Cliff and Grandma were like two old buddies. They even exchanged cell phone numbers.

When we got off the plane, we had to show our passports to the security officers. People were in a big long line waiting to go through to get their luggage. That's when Becky and Mindy noticed Mrs. Cliff.

"Did you see that your teacher is here?" Becky said.

"I know. She sat next to Grandma the entire flight."

"This is too good," Mindy said. "I can't believe it!"

"You can't believe it? This was supposed to be a week off from school, and now Mrs. Cliff is here in Aruba with me, and she's staying at our hotel."

"I love it!" Becky said.

When it was our time to go through customs, a lady looked at each of our pictures on our passports and then said our names and asked us a few questions. She looked at me and said, "What's your name?"

"I'm Justin."

"Welcome to Aruba, Justin. Are you ready to have fun this week?"

"I was until I realized my teacher is here too. Is there any way I can take another flight back to New York?"

"Justin, stop being so dramatic," Mom said. "Big deal, your teacher is here. There'll be so many people at the hotel, I bet you don't even see her again this whole trip."

"You're all set. You can walk toward the door and pick up your luggage. Taxis are waiting outside. Good luck trying to avoid your teacher," the lady said with a smirk.

"Thanks," I said.

We walked over by the luggage machine, and some bags were starting to come out. I could feel the warm air coming in from outside and see the trees blowing in the breeze.

"It's going to be a wonderful time, Justin," Mom said. "Look how lovely it looks outside. Just relax."

That's when Grandma appeared. "I told Gertrude she can hop in a taxi with us to head over to the hotel. The poor dear is all alone."

"Who's Gertrude?" Dad asked.

"Justin's teacher. She's a real darling."

"Grandma, no offense, but I didn't really expect to come here and hang out with my teacher," I said.

"I know you didn't, sugar, but that's exactly what's happened, so we're going to be polite and make the best of it."

Mrs. Cliff walked up with her bags. "Justin will grab those for you, Mrs. Gerty," Grandma said. "Justin, give your teacher a little help."

This isn't happening, I thought as I picked up her bags and made my way toward the exit.

Mindy took a picture of me. "This is going to be a Christmas to remember," she said.

"Maybe you two can get your hair braided together?" Becky snickered.

"Very funny," I said. "You can put that on the list of things that will definitely not happen this week."

"We'll see," Mindy said.

13
Lizard Mania

We all piled into a big van, and I sat in the back with the girls, and Grandma and Mrs. Cliff sat up front. I realized having Mrs. Cliff at the hotel was only going to be half my problem. The girls were going to have a field day with this and drive me completely crazy. They said they were going to take as many pictures of me and Mrs. Cliff together as possible and make me a memory album. I complained to Mom, and she said she didn't want to hear it.

When we finally got to the hotel, it was about twelve. The front desk told Grandma and Dad that our rooms wouldn't be ready until four. It was fine with me because all I wanted to do was head down to the pool or the beach.

Dad gave the front desk his cell phone number, and they told him they'd call when our room was ready.

Mom said, "We're going to head to the pool and the beach for the rest of the day, so let's get our bathing suits out of our bags and store our luggage with the front desk."

"You can store your things in my room," Mrs. Cliff offered. "It's ready now, and I'm going to head up there and do a little reading or maybe take a nap."

"That's nice of you, Mrs. Cliff," Mom said, "but we'll be fine leaving our things down here, and then we won't bother you later if we need anything out of our bags."

"Suit yourself. Thanks for sharing your taxi with me. I'll see you later on, Mimi?" she said to Grandma.

"You better believe it, Gertrude," Grandma said.

Mrs. Cliff left, and I was relaxed for the first time all day. We all changed and walked out toward the pool. The place was like paradise. There were palm trees and paths leading every which way. The pool was at the bottom of the paths, and past the pool was a long stretch of white sand beach and crystal-clear water. We were on a path for less than a minute when I spotted a pretty big bluish lizard scurrying across the grass. I lunged for it, but it was way too fast.

"Oh no," Becky said. "You're going to go crazy in this place. I bet there are lizards everywhere."

I hadn't really had time to think about the fact that we were in the Caribbean and the place was crawling with lizards. I wondered if I could sneak a few new pets back home on the plane. I was wondering how I'd accomplish that without hurting the lizard or getting in some kind of trouble, when I spotted a huge iguana, which would cost a bunch of money at a pet store, just hanging out right on the path.

"You're going to love it here," Dad said. "They're everywhere!"

He was right too. There seemed to be lizards everywhere I looked. It was like a dream come true.

"Can I hang out over here by the trees and bushes and try to catch some?" I asked.

"I don't see why not," Mom said. "I'll grab a chair over there, where we can see each other, and I'll relax and read for a while. You do whatever you need to do. Just promise to stay in this area."

The girls and Grandma headed for the pool, and Dad went for a swim in the sea. I had to admit, it was an amazing way to spend Christmas Day. It was like a reptile lover's dream come true.

Finally, I thought, *things are going my way.*

14
Dive Bomb

A t four o'clock, the front desk called Dad to tell him the room was ready. We grabbed our things and one of those hotel luggage carts and headed up to our rooms. Grandma had booked two rooms next to each other that connected. She and the girls were staying in one room, and I was staying in the other with Mom and Dad, which I was happy about because I didn't have to sleep in the same room as the girls.

The first night we went to sleep pretty early because we were all so tired from the trip. The next morning I woke up really early and wanted to go out to start looking for critters. I couldn't wait to check out down by the beach. If there were that many lizards just around the hotel, I couldn't imagine the cool stuff I'd find by the beach.

Mom and Dad were still sleeping, but I could hear Grandma humming next door, so I tapped lightly on the door.

She opened up and said, "I'm headed down to the beach to reserve some lounge chairs for us. Want to come?"

"Sure," I said, grabbing my video camera.

"I might have to wait on line for a while. They said at the front desk that the line can be long. They don't open for another half hour."

I didn't mind. I figured that while Grandma waited on line, I could look for critters.

When we got down to the beach, there were about thirty people waiting for beach chairs. Mrs. Cliff walked up at the exact same time as us and got on line with Grandma.

"Hi, Justin," she said.

"Hi, Mrs. Cliff," I managed. "How'd you get here at the same exact time as us?"

"I texted her," Grandma said. "We're going to spend the day together."

"Wonderful," I said. "My grandma and my teacher hanging out all day, what more could a kid my age wish for?"

"Justin, don't be rude," Grandma said. I noticed she was a little different around Mrs. Cliff, and I didn't like it.

"I don't mean to be rude. It's just..."

"It's just that you're embarrassed," Mrs. Cliff said.

"I'm not embarrassed. It's just that I was kind of looking forward to a break from you...I mean from school. That's all. Don't all kids want a break from school and their teachers?"

"I loved my teachers growing up," Grandma said. "I don't think you give Mrs. Cliff the respect she deserves. Maybe we can work on that this week, and it will carry over into class when you return."

"I don't see that happening," I said.

"Justin!" Grandma said. "What's gotten into you?"

"Nothing, I'm just talking and trying to be honest."

"Why don't you go look for your lizards while we wait on the line?"

I couldn't believe Grandma was hanging out with Mrs. Cliff and was upset with me. If anyone should have been upset, it should have been me for having to hang out with my teacher during the break.

I tried catching a few lizards and then decided to take a break because it was already super hot. They had a cold water station set up with a bunch of comfy lounge chairs. I was lying on a lounge chair, waiting for Grandma and Mrs. Cliff, when I heard a man shriek. I sat up fast and saw him on one of the paths, running and holding his head. He was looking around like something had fallen on him.

I noticed a woman walking from the beach onto the same path. She made it about halfway down, and a small black bird swooped down from a palm tree and pecked her on the top of the head. She ran down the length of the rest of the path as the man before her had. She wasn't hurt or anything, but it looked like it surprised her pretty good. It looked pretty funny, like the sort of thing I'd seen on the Internet or those funny video shows. There was a lady sitting on a chair near me, and she started to laugh too.

A third person started down the path, and I decided to take out the video camera. It was hysterical. The man made it about halfway, and the same bird darted out of the palm tree and buzzed his head. He ran as the other two had before him. Only this time, I got it on film. He was laughing the entire time, so it mustn't have hurt. A few more people gathered near where I was sitting and prepared for the next person to walk down the path. It was like being in on a practical joke.

One of the people watching said the bird was probably protecting a nest. Everyone seemed to agree, but no one seemed interested in warning the people coming down the path.

I couldn't believe my eyes when I noticed Mrs. Cliff strolling along the path, headed toward where the bird was dive-bombing. It was too perfect. I pointed my video camera on her. Aaron and the guys at school wouldn't believe this if I tried to explain it to them, so I was so glad I'd brought the camera. Mrs. Cliff was not paying attention to where she was going because she was trying to read something on her phone as she walked. When she was halfway up the path, the bird flew out of the tree, but this time it wasn't taking any prisoners. It dove toward the top of her head and crashed into her pretty hard. It pecked at the top of her head while hovering above her for a few seconds. She shrieked out and ran for cover. Instead of running down the path like the other people before her had done, she turned and started heading across the grass in my direction. Through my video camera, I watched Mrs. Cliff stumbling toward me and screaming at the top of her lungs. It was so loud that it echoed through the resort, and people started coming out onto their balconies. Several people went over to Mrs. Cliff to see if she was OK. I don't know why I didn't stop taping, but I just kept on rolling.

Before I knew it, Grandma was behind me and said, "What are you doing?"

"I was just watching this bird dive-bomb people going by."

"And you decided to videotape it instead of warning them?"

"Well, the first few people didn't get hurt or anything. They just ran down the path to get away. It was really funny."

"And you saw this and didn't warn Mrs. Cliff?"

I don't think there'd ever been a time when Grandma was mad at me before this trip, and now she seemed really upset with me. I was so mad at Mrs. Cliff for being there.

"I'm surprised and, frankly, a little disappointed in you, Justin," Grandma said.

I noticed Mindy and Becky out on their balcony taking pictures of me. One of the women from the hotel brought Mrs. Cliff an ice pack and apologized.

"It's all right," Mrs. Cliff said. "It was just a passionate mother bird protecting her nest. I suggest the hotel tape off the area to protect the birds."

The woman agreed and left to go get some help. Grandma suggested that I stay and help the lady to make up for my poor decision.

"I don't mind helping," I said.

"Good, I'll sit down over here with Mrs. Cliff and order an iced coffee. When you're done, I'll bring you back up to the room."

They grabbed a table and talked to one of the waitresses. I stood waiting for the lady to come back and had what seemed to be a great idea. I figured that if it was funny watching other people get attacked by the little bird, it would probably be hysterical to take video of myself being attacked. I ran to the end of the path and turned on the video camera. Then I walked along the path and waited for the bird to strike. A few people were watching and waiting for me to get nabbed. I didn't see it at all—until I felt it collide with the top of my head. Its beak scraped along the top of my head like a sharp stick. I fell to my knees, and it struck again. I was laughing because it didn't hurt that bad, but I was also a little frightened because it seemed to be going at me extra hard.

When I stood up and ran down the path, it hovered right in front of me and pecked at my cheeks. Each time it pecked, it was like getting a shot in the face. It got so bad that I stopped taping and wrapped my arms over my head for protection. It felt as if there were a few birds because the pecking was getting worse. That's when someone threw a towel over my head, grabbed my hand, and led me to the end of the path and safety. I was relieved because it was getting scary there for a minute. When I stopped and pulled the towel off my face, I realized Mrs. Cliff had saved me.

Grandma ran over and said, "My goodness. What would you do without this woman, Justin? She just saved your life. Those birds were pecking at you like you were dipped in honey!"

I touched my cheek and realized I was bleeding.

"Let's get you back to the room," Grandma said. "Your cheeks look like Swiss cheese. We've got to get some medication on those cuts right away. Your mother is not going to be happy."

15
Trust Me

When I looked in the mirror back at the room, I couldn't believe it. My face was covered in little scratches and cuts from where the birds had pecked at my face. The girls told me I looked like I'd fallen on a porcupine.

"I'm sorry if I'm ruining the trip," I said to Grandma later that night at dinner.

"You could never ruin the trip," Grandma said. "I booked this trip because I never get to really spend time with you kids. I'll tell you something, though," she said seriously. "You always seem to be complaining about school and how horrible it is. Maybe you need to stop blaming Mrs. Cliff and start taking responsibility yourself."

"I know you like her," I said, "but trust me, her class is a nightmare."

"You mean the woman who saved your life earlier today?"

"Trust me, the only reason she saved my life in the first place is so she can keep on ruining it at school."

16
No Worries

Things got pretty calm toward the middle of the week. I was finally starting to feel relaxed and enjoy myself. I rented WaveRunners with Dad one day, went snorkeling with the whole family another, and got much better at catching the lizards. Mrs. Cliff seemed to keep to herself after the bird attack incident. She must have needed a break from me as much as I needed one from her.

On Thursday, we were all hanging out on the beach. Mrs. Cliff joined us because she'd been shopping earlier in the day with Grandma. I was trying to catch a crab I'd seen pop its head out of the sand a few times. The adults were all talking about how fast the week was going and how busy they'd be when they got back to work.

Becky and Mindy were reading. "I'm just about done with the book my teacher assigned me over the break," Mindy said.

"Me too," Becky said.

"Didn't you have an assignment you were supposed to work on this week?" Mom asked me.

"Yeah," I said.

"I haven't seen you working on it at all. Where is it?"

"I kind of forgot it at home. I guess I'll have to do it when I get back."

Mrs. Cliff definitely heard, and I could tell she wanted to say something.

"Mrs. Cliff," Mom said, sitting up, "I hate to ask you a teacher question on your vacation, but is the packet something Justin can complete when we get home?"

"It would be extremely difficult to do it well in such a short period of time. It is intended to be worked on a little at a time over the course of the week."

"Justin," Dad said, "I know we left in a hurry, but that was important and your responsibility to bring."

"I have an extra copy in my room," Mrs. Cliff said. "You're welcome to it."

I couldn't believe my luck. I'd forgotten that packet on purpose, and now she had an extra in her room.

"That's wonderful," Grandma said.

"Yes, wonderful," I said sarcastically.

17
Grounded In Paradise

That night Mom and Dad took the girls out for a fancy dinner, and I had to stay in the room with Grandma to work on my packet. The next morning, which was our second-to-last day at the hotel, Mom and Dad told me I had to stay in the room until the packet was done. They let me use Mindy's laptop so I could research the different holidays, and Mom, Dad, and Grandma took turns hanging out with me in the room.

When it was Mom's turn, she gave me this really long lecture about being responsible.

She kept ranting on about the way the girls take care of their own things, get their schoolwork done on their own, and stay out of trouble. The last one was a total joke because the only reason the girls stay out of trouble is they're really good at not getting caught. When I said that to Mom, she got really mad at me.

"It's true," I said. "They're always picking on me and making fun of me, and you guys never say anything."

"I think you're just looking for something to blame other than yourself. You're the one who forgot your packet, you're the one who allowed your teacher and yourself to get pecked half to death by birds, and you're the one who told your teacher she was awful on the last day of school. Whose fault is all of that?" Mom asked.

"Mine, I guess," I said.

"You're going to be in fifth grade next year, Justin. It's time you start acting a little more mature. How are you doing on that packet?"

"I'm not even half done. Can't I do it when we get home?"

"I'm afraid not. Your father and I decided that it's your most important priority and you can do other things once it's completed."

"So I'm grounded even though we're in a tropical paradise?" I asked.

"Yep," Mom said, flipping through a magazine.

I was so mad it was hard to concentrate. There were so many amazing things I could have been doing out on the beach or by the pool, and I was stuck because of Mrs. Cliff.

18
I Wonder Where He Learned That?

At lunchtime, Mom told me to take a break, and we went down to meet everyone for lunch. I asked her if we could stop to see the exotic birds.

"Yes," she said. "It's right down next to the convenience store. I'll run in and grab a few things, and you can check out the birds."

Finally, I thought, *something fun.* I walked over to an area toward the back of the lobby where they had parrots in large cages. Mom went into the store and told me not to leave the area.

The parrots were so cool. Some of them talked too. There was one that said, "Hey, how's it goin'?" It was pretty funny.

"Pretty terrible, thanks for asking," I said.

The bird repeated, "Hey, how's it goin'?"

"I told you already," I said. "Pretty terrible. My annoying teacher, Mrs. Cliff, is here, and I wish *she'd* just leave me alone already. She drives me crazy."

One of the other birds repeated, "My annoying teacher, Mrs. Cliff."

I laughed. It was pretty awesome. I turned on my video camera and pointed it at the birds. "Mrs. Cliff is totally annoying," I said.

The bird repeated, "Mrs. Cliff is totally annoying."

I kept taping. *Aaron and the guys at school are going to love this*, I thought.

I taped it a few different times. Each time it made me laugh. I couldn't wait to get home and edit the videos together. Then I noticed Grandma and Mrs. Cliff coming toward the bird area. I tried to walk back and cut them off, but they said they wanted to check out the birds too.

"Your mom asked us to come get you for lunch. These birds are simply miraculous," Grandma said.

"I'd love a bird," Mrs. Cliff said, "but they're so much work."

"And they live a long life. It's not a small commitment. You don't want to get a beautiful creature like this and then regret it," Grandma said, turning to me. "Speaking of regretting things, I just realized you never apologized for letting Mrs. Cliff get attacked by those birds the other day."

I tried to look as sorry as possible.

"Justin," Grandma said, "I think you owe Mrs. Cliff an apology."

"It would have been nice if you'd warned me," Mrs. Cliff said. "It cut the top of my head with its beak. It was very frightening."

"I didn't think you'd get hurt," I said. "It looked funny when the other people walked through."

"Justin," Grandma said again, "what do you have to say to Mrs. Cliff?"

I knew I had to apologize no matter how badly I didn't want to. Grandma was getting more and more annoyed with every passing second, but I was having a hard time making myself apologize. *She should be the one apologizing to me,* I thought. She should have never even been on our trip.

"Justin, what do you want to say to Mrs. Cliff?" Grandma said one last time.

I was just about to apologize when one of the parrots said, "Mrs. Cliff is totally annoying." He didn't say it once either. He kept repeating it over and over: "Mrs. Cliff is totally annoying. Mrs. Cliff is totally annoying. Mrs. Cliff is totally annoying."

"I wonder where he learned that," I said, trying to look surprised. I'd never seen Grandma so frustrated.

19
Just Send It

By the time the last day of the trip rolled around, I had completely broken down. I couldn't wait for the trip and the winter break to be over. It had been a total nightmare with Mrs. Cliff. All I wanted to do was get home to my pets and my room and forget the whole trip ever happened.

I finished my packet on the plane back to New York. I sat in between Grandma and Mrs. Cliff because Mrs. Cliff wanted the window seat and Grandma wanted the aisle. They were done caring about what I wanted. Everyone was upset with me.

I think even the stewardess was mad at me. When I was taping Mrs. Cliff snoring, the stewardess leaned in and said, "I think it's rude to tape other people sleeping."

"She doesn't mind," I said.

"But I do," she said sternly, so I shut off the video camera, but not before getting some awesome tape of Mrs. Cliff sawing some wood.

After the long flight and another scary ride in Norton's danger van, I was ready for some calm. Mom, Dad, and Grandma unpacked and plunked down on the couch. The girls called all their friends, and I headed straight to my room and hopped on the computer. I loaded up all the video from the trip and started editing it together.

I had a ton of video of the resort, the beach, and the pool. I also had a bunch of really funny clips of Mrs. Cliff: the bird attack, the parrot saying, "Mrs. Cliff is annoying," and her snoring on the plane ride home. I edited them together.

Aaron called to see how the trip was and to welcome me home. He'd been taking care of my snakes and feeding my turkey while we were away. I told him all about the trip. He said his mom told him he didn't have to do the packet and she would write him a note for Mrs. Cliff. I couldn't believe that I had been grounded in Aruba to finish the silly packet and his mom didn't even care if he did it or not.

"I can't believe your mom grounded you while you were on vacation! And totally can't believe Mrs. Cliff hung out with your family the whole time. Who has worse luck than you?"

"Probably no one," I said. "I did get some amazing video of Mrs. Cliff, though."

When I told him about it, he begged me to send it to him.

"I'll send it," I said, "but you have to promise to not share it."

"I promise. Just send it!"

I sent it and then jumped into my own bed, happy to be home at last.

20
It's Totally Not My Fault!

O n New Year's Eve, we stayed home and
hung out with Grandma. We ordered in
takeout and watched the ball drop on TV. After
midnight, Grandma told me New Year's Eve is a
time for making changes and setting goals for
the coming New Year.

"I think this is an opportunity for you to set
some goals for yourself," she said.

"What kind of goals?" I asked.

"You know what I'm talking about. You're
getting older. You can't go through your whole

school life complaining about everything. School can be a rewarding experience, but you have to give it a chance."

"I guess you're right," I said. "I could try to be a little more positive."

"You could try to be a lot more positive. I think you should also try to keep yourself out of trouble. You're a good boy. There's no reason you should be causing trouble at school. That needs to stop."

"I'll try, Grandma," I said.

"Thank you, sweetheart." Her phone buzzed. Her face looked concerned as she read the text.

I took a handful of pretzels and sat back on the couch. She was right. Maybe I had been being too negative at school and getting into too much trouble.

"Justin," she said, sounding concerned, "Mrs. Cliff just texted me. There seems to be a video of her from Aruba posted on the Internet. Do you know how it got there?"

"Maybe," I said. "But it's totally not my fault!"

www.raymondbean.com

Raymond Bean books

Baseball: A Ticket to the Bigs

<u>Sweet Farts Series</u>
Sweet Farts #1
Sweet Farts #2 Rippin' It Old School
Sweet Farts #3 Blown Away

<u>School Is A Nightmare Series</u>
School Is A Nightmare #1
First Week, Worst Week
School Is A Nightmare #2 The Field Trip
School Is A Nightmare #3 Shocktober
School Is A Nightmare #4
Yuck Mouth and the Thanksgiving Miracle
School Is A Nightmare – Quadzilla
(Books 1-4) Special Edition
School Is A Nightmare #5
Winter Breakdown (Coming Fall 2013)
School Is A Nightmare #6 Cupid's Crush
(Coming Winter 2014)

50876236R00056

Made in the USA
Charleston, SC
10 January 2016